Goldilocks a
Three Bears

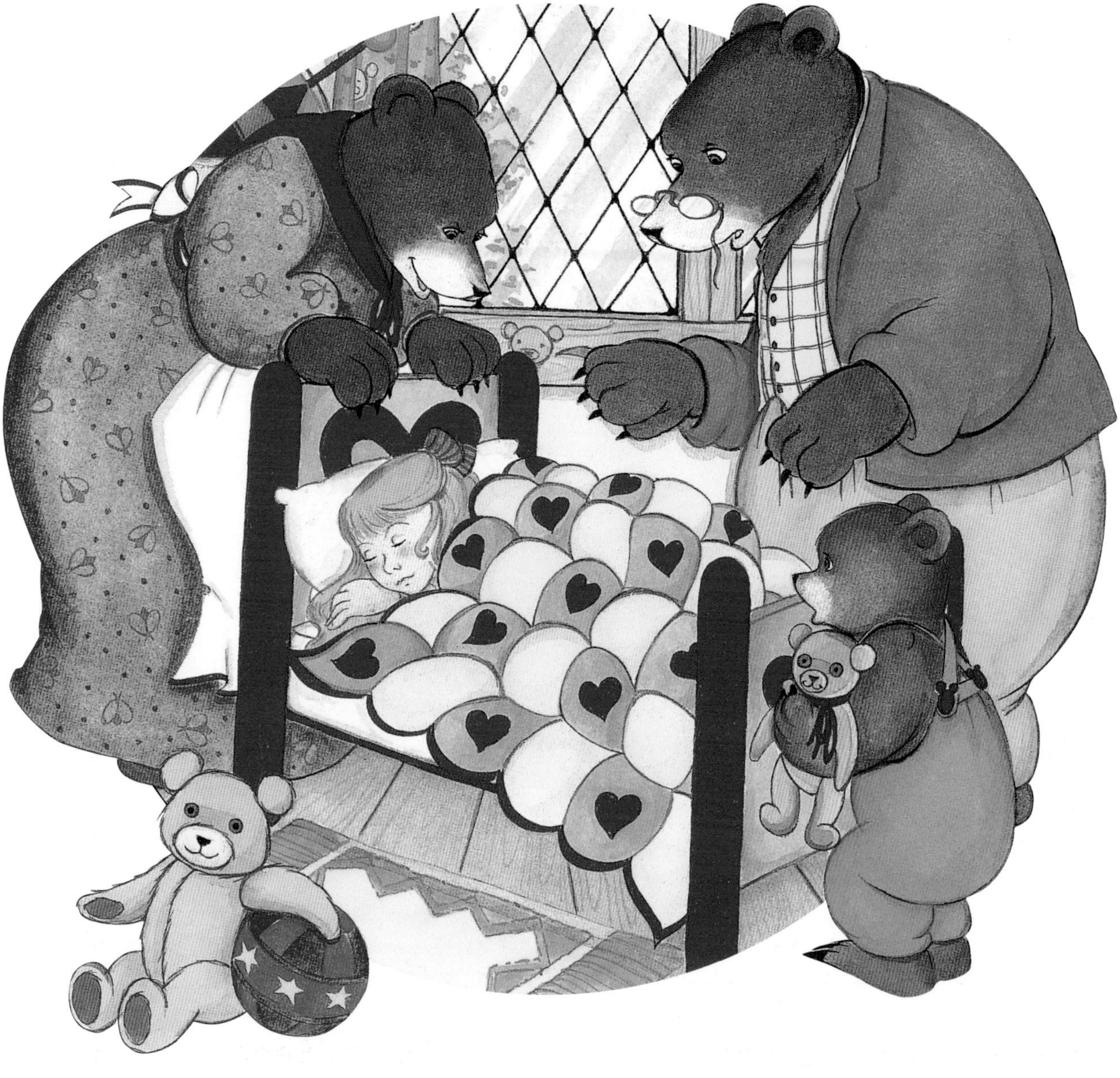

Award Publications Limited

This book belongs to:

....

Once upon a time, there were three 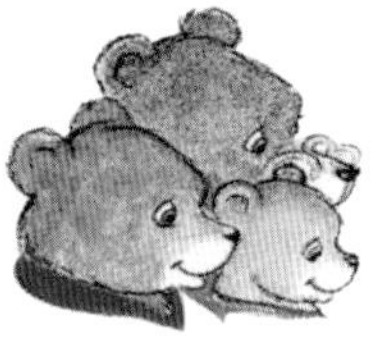 who lived in a 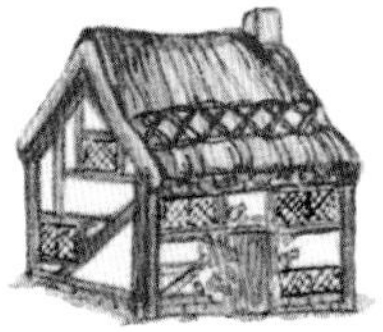 deep in the 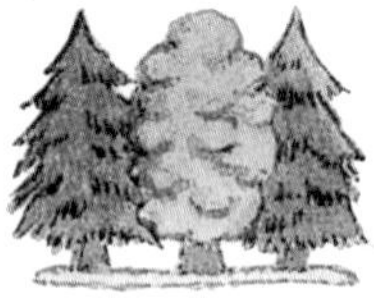.

There was a great big and gruff 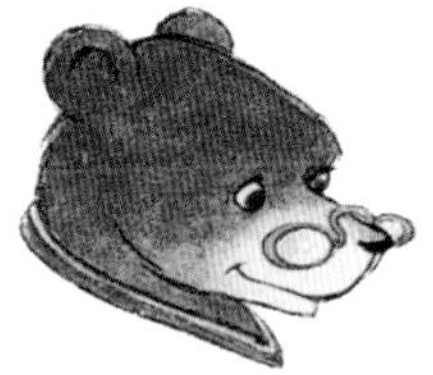. There was a gentle, middle-sized 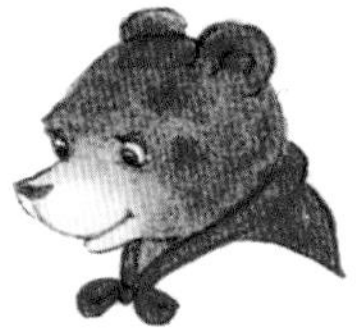 and there was also a dear little 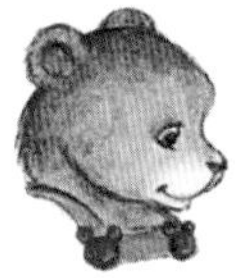.

One fine morning, 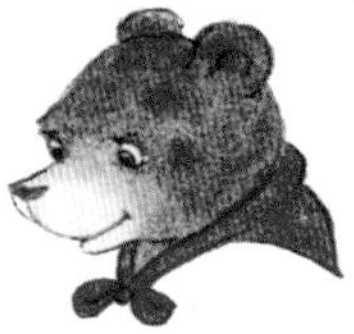 made some porridge for breakfast.

She poured it into three different sized 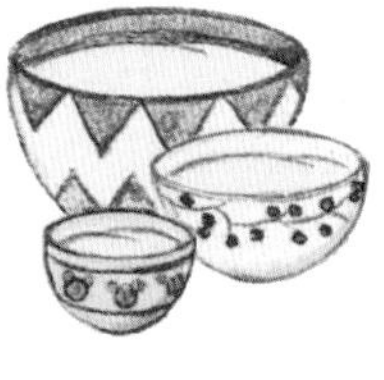 to cool.

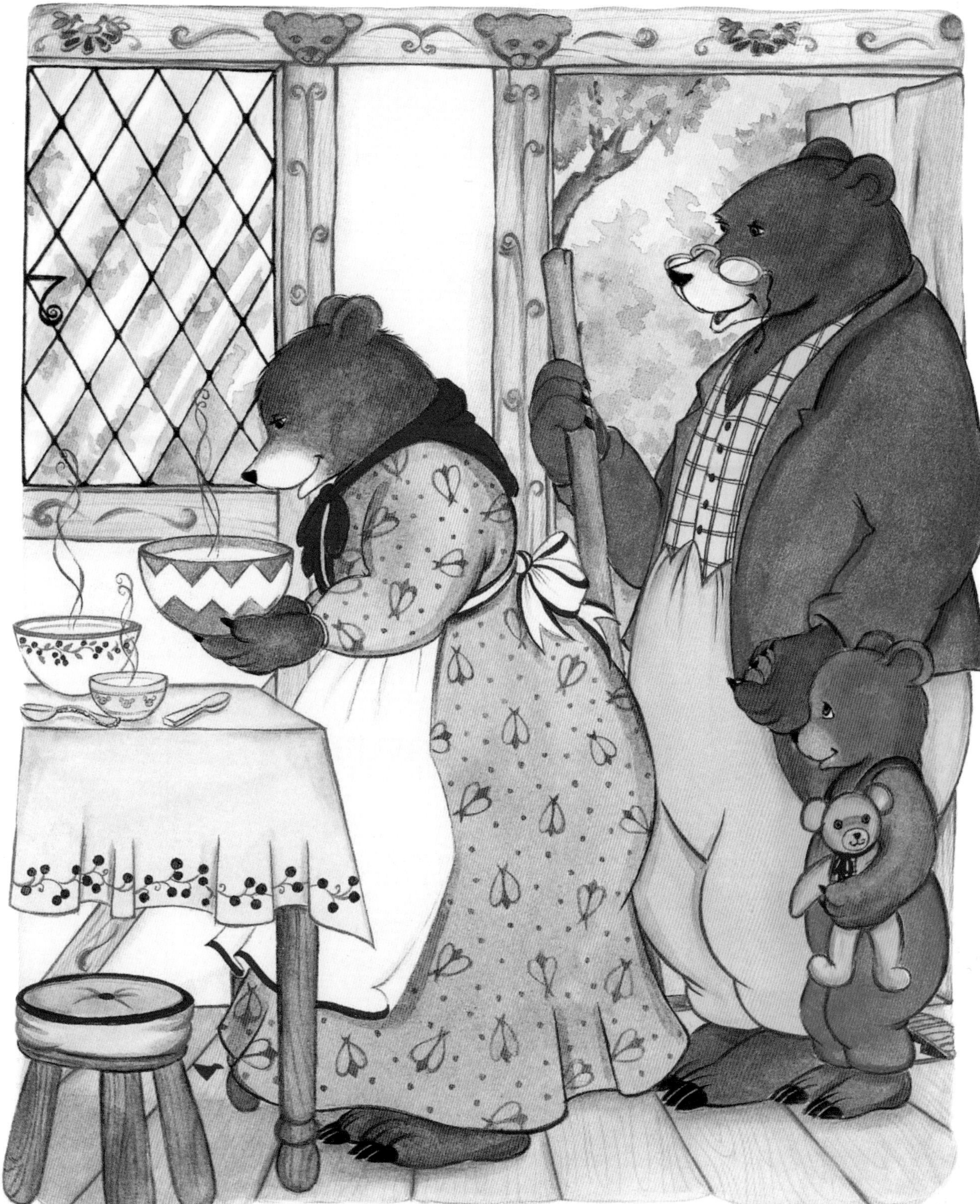

The three 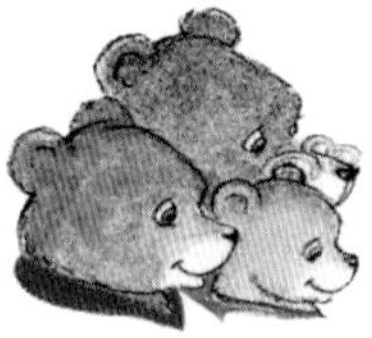 then set out for a walk in the 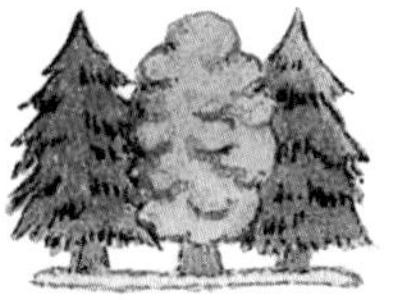.

While they were gone, a little 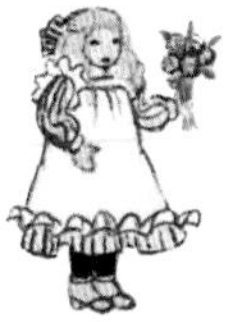 knocked on their 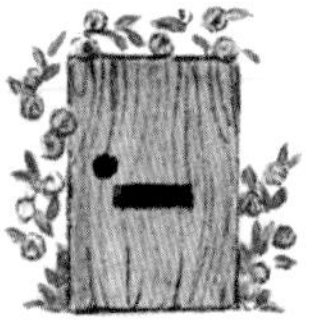. Her name was 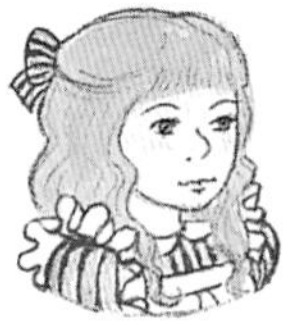 and she had been out gathering 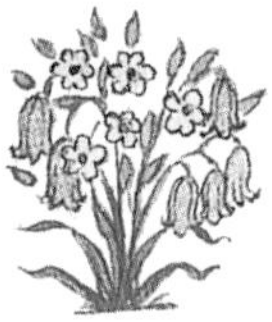.

When nobody answered, she peeped inside the 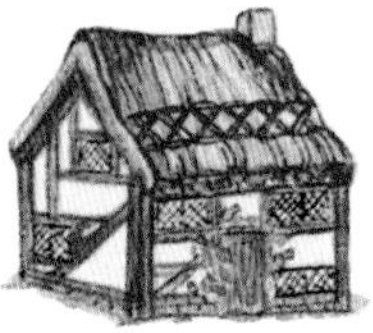 and saw three 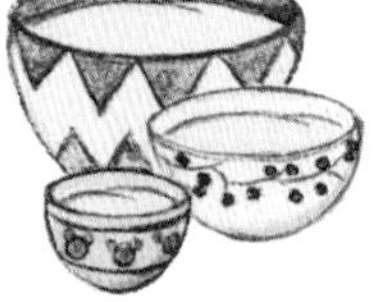 of porridge on the 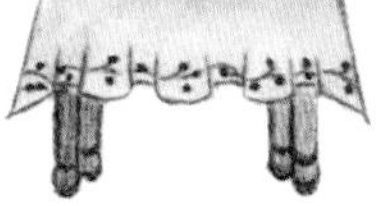.

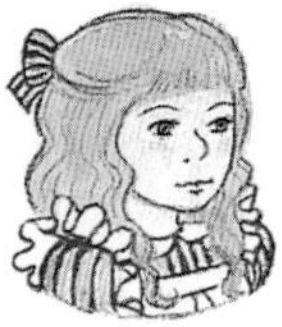 was very hungry. She tasted the steaming porridge in the 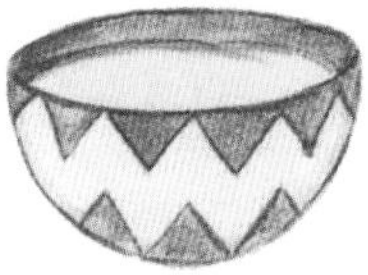. It was too hot.

She tasted the porridge in the 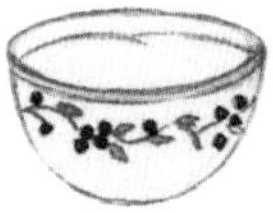. It was much too cold.

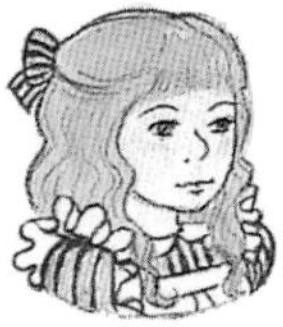 then tasted the porridge in the 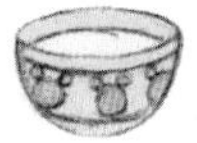. It was just right, and before she could stop herself, 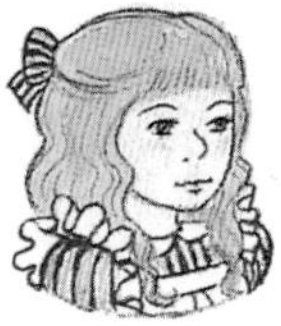 had eaten up all the porridge in the 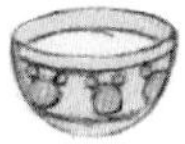.

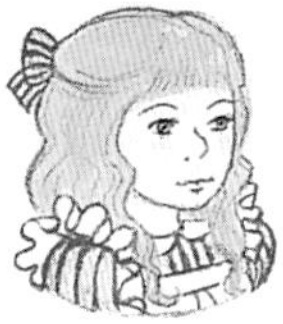 saw three 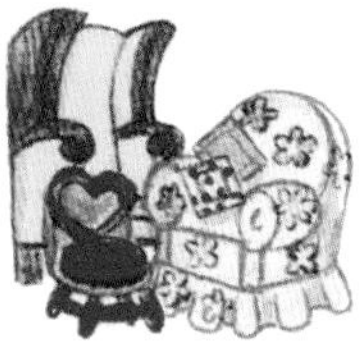 in the room. There was a great 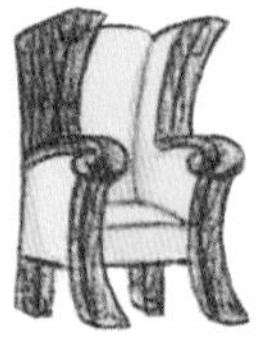 for 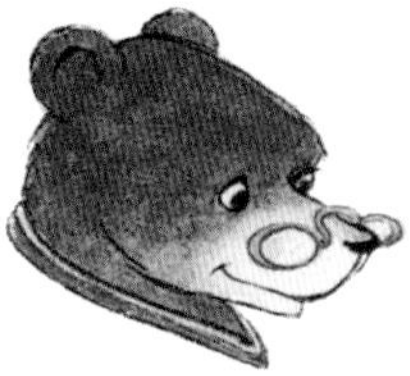. There was a 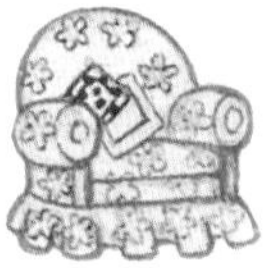 for 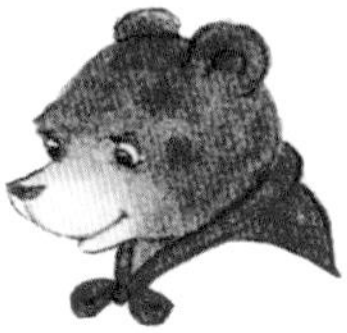 and a 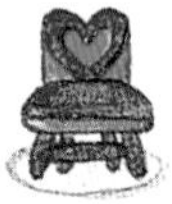 for 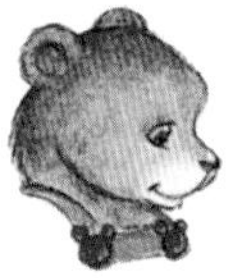.

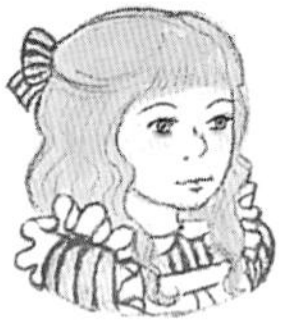 sat down on the 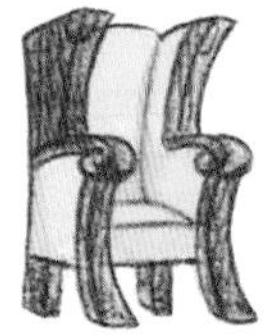, but it was much too hard. Then she sat on the 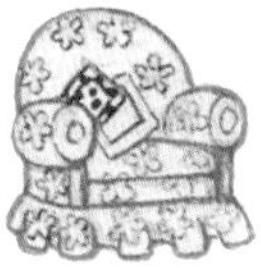, but that was far too soft.

When 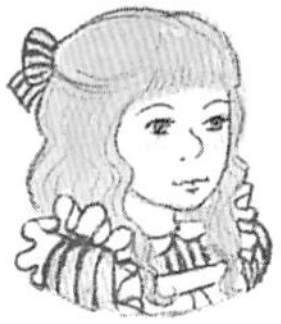 sat on the 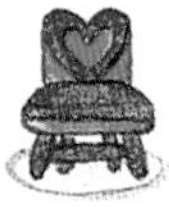, it was not too hard, or too soft. She found it was just right.

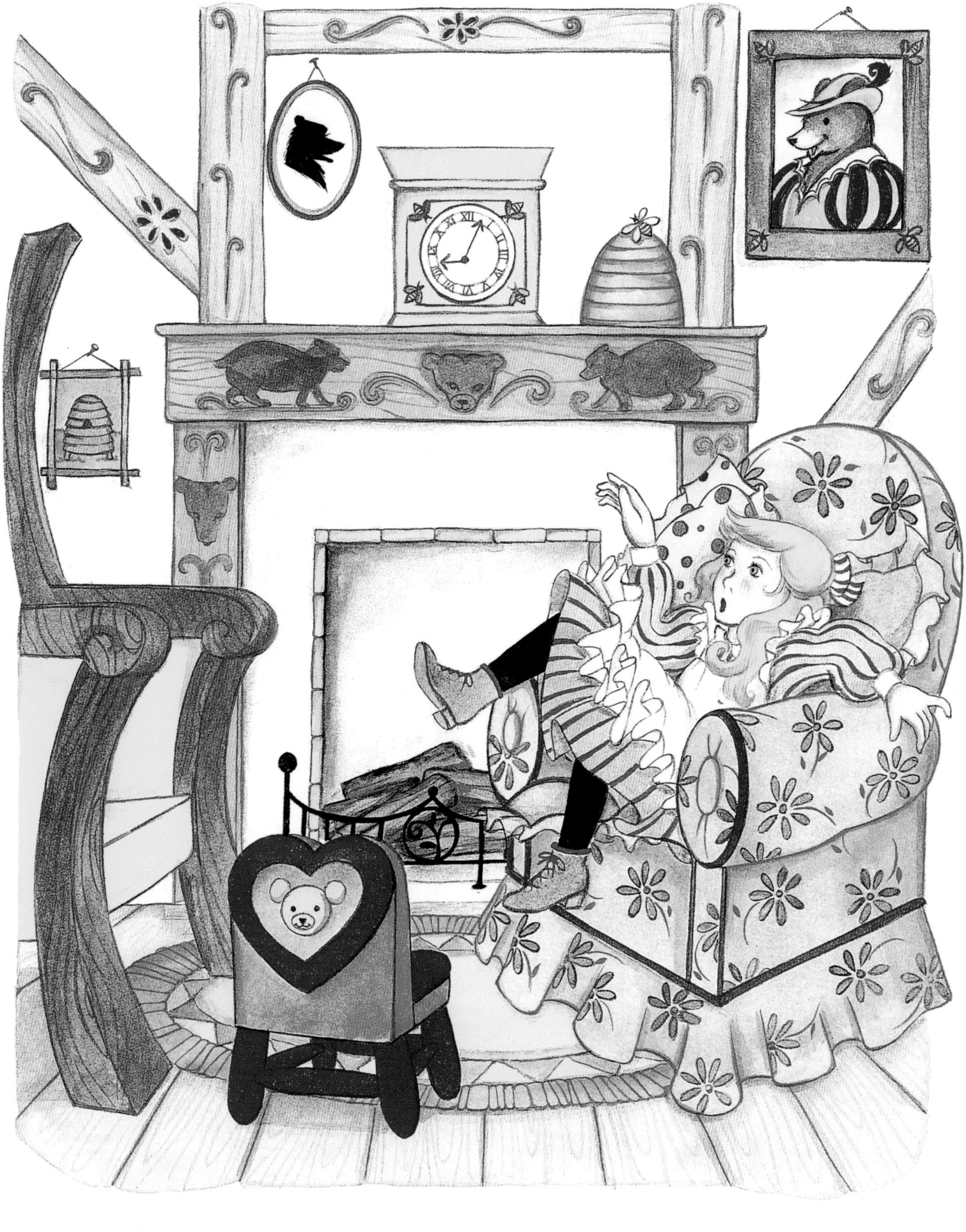

But 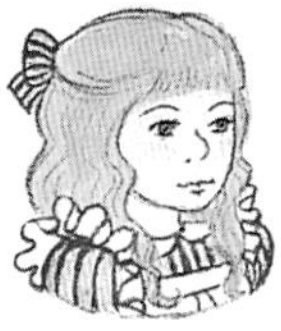 was much too big and heavy for such a 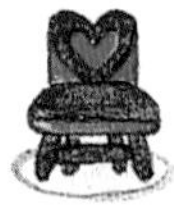. It broke into 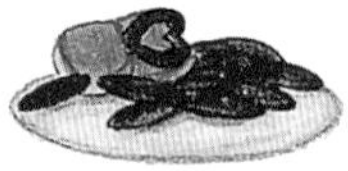.

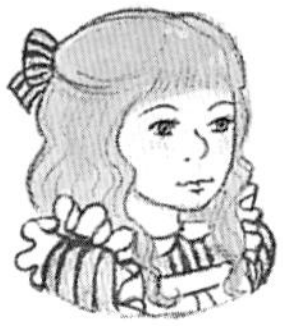 picked herself up and then decided to go and see what was up the 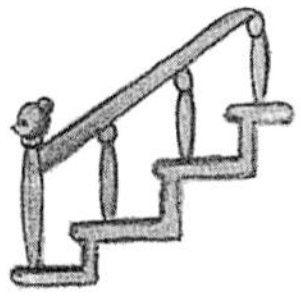.

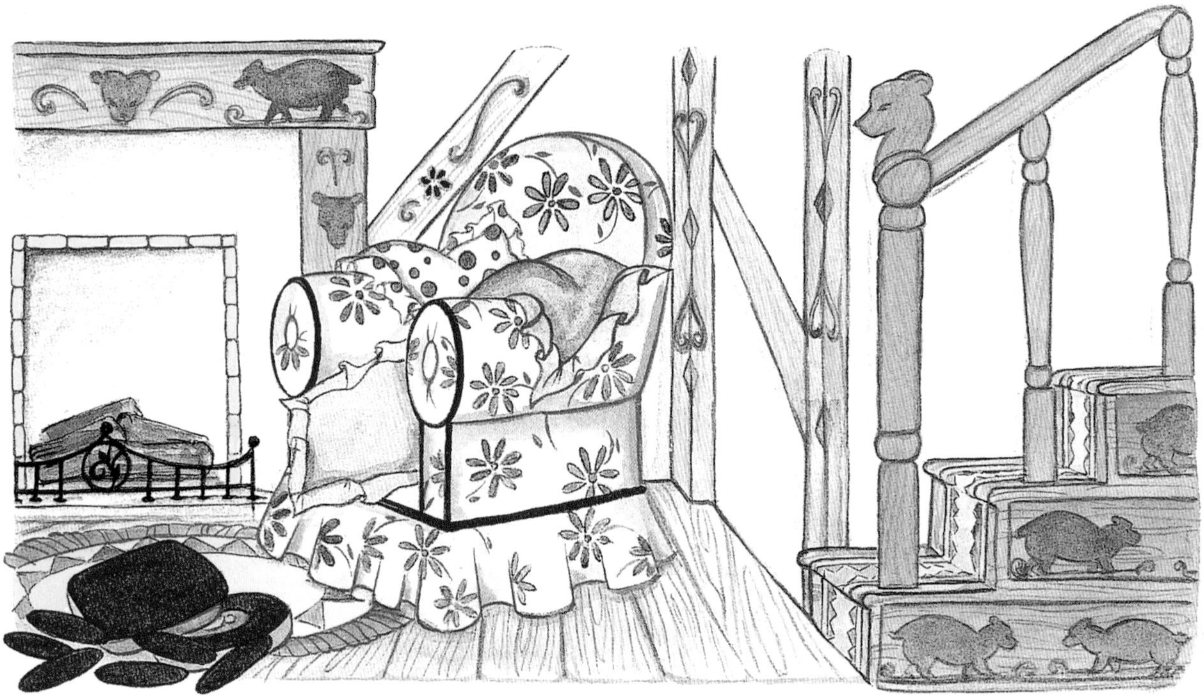

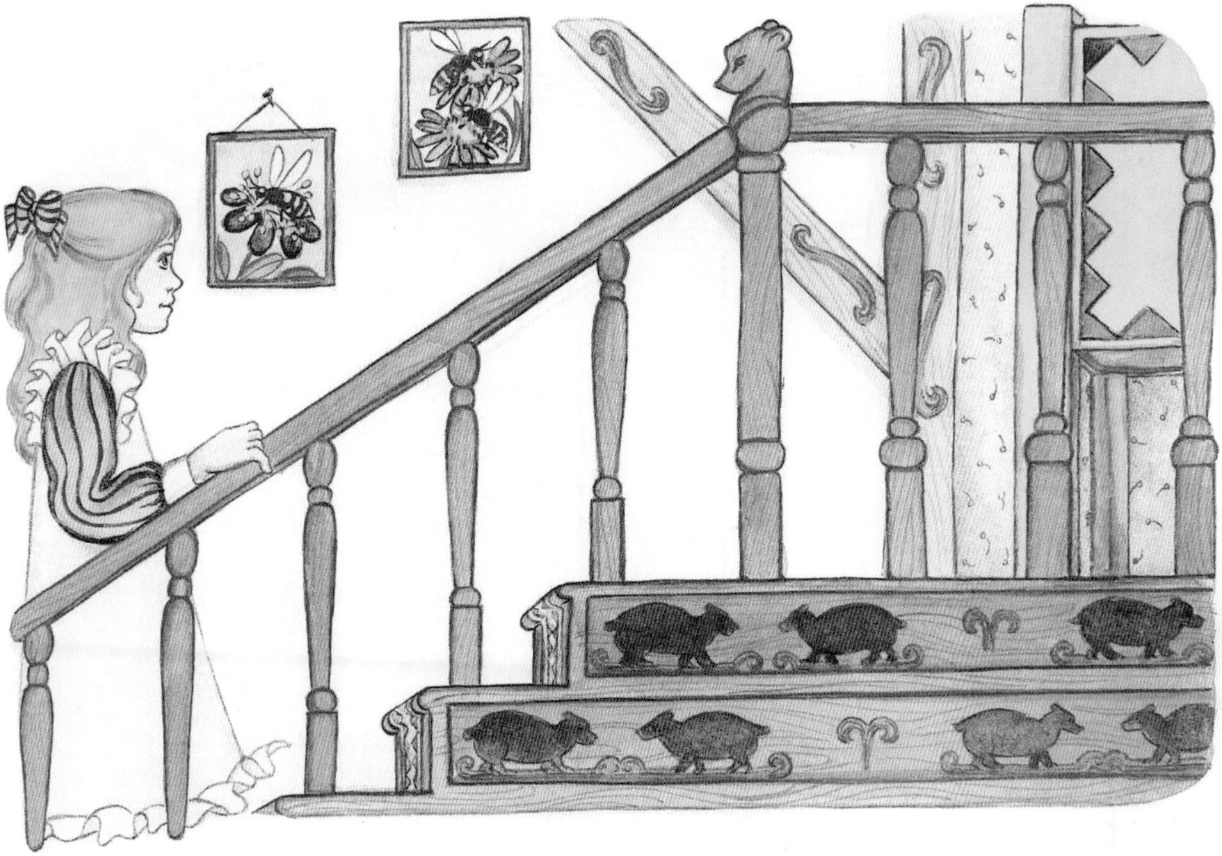

She found three 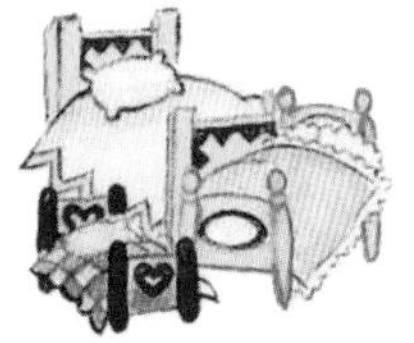 .

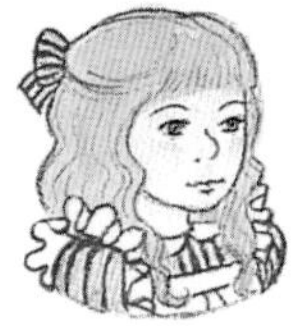 was now very sleepy, so she tried to climb on to the great 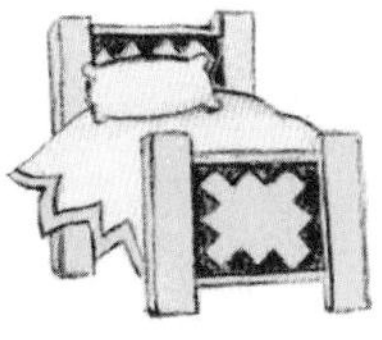 , which belonged to 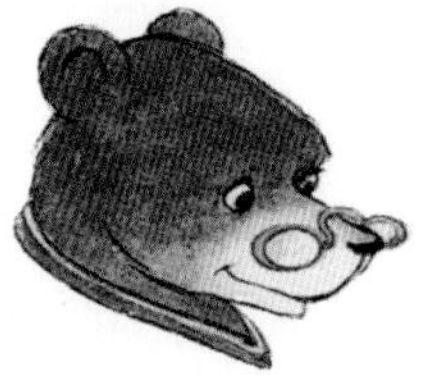 .

It was too high.

Next, 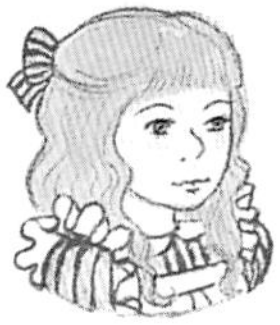 lay down on the 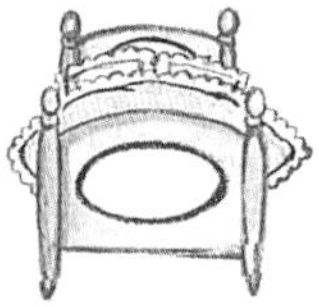, which belonged to 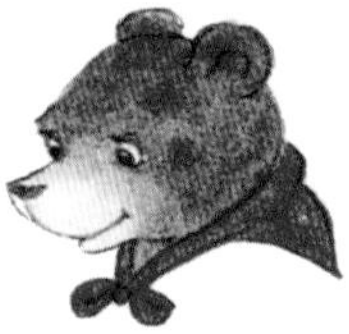. It was very soft and she sank down much too low.

Yawning, 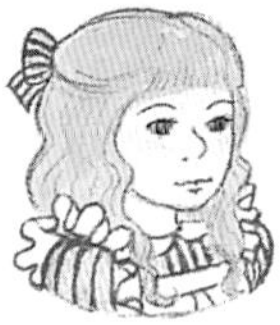 climbed into the 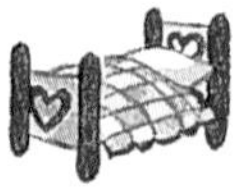, which belonged to 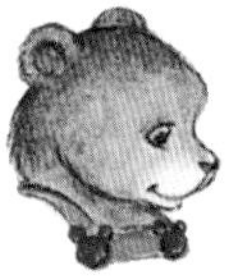. She found this 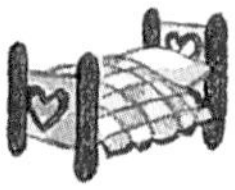 was cosy and snug and felt just right.

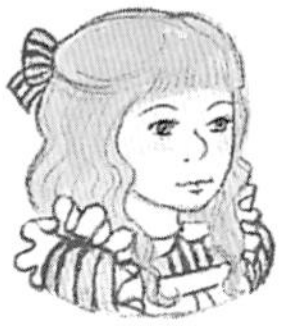 was soon fast asleep, so she did not hear the three 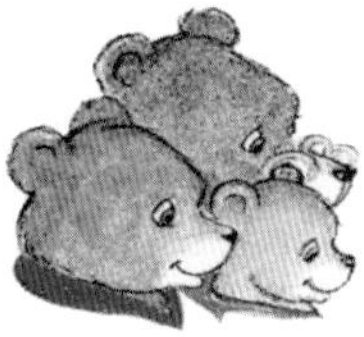 come back home.

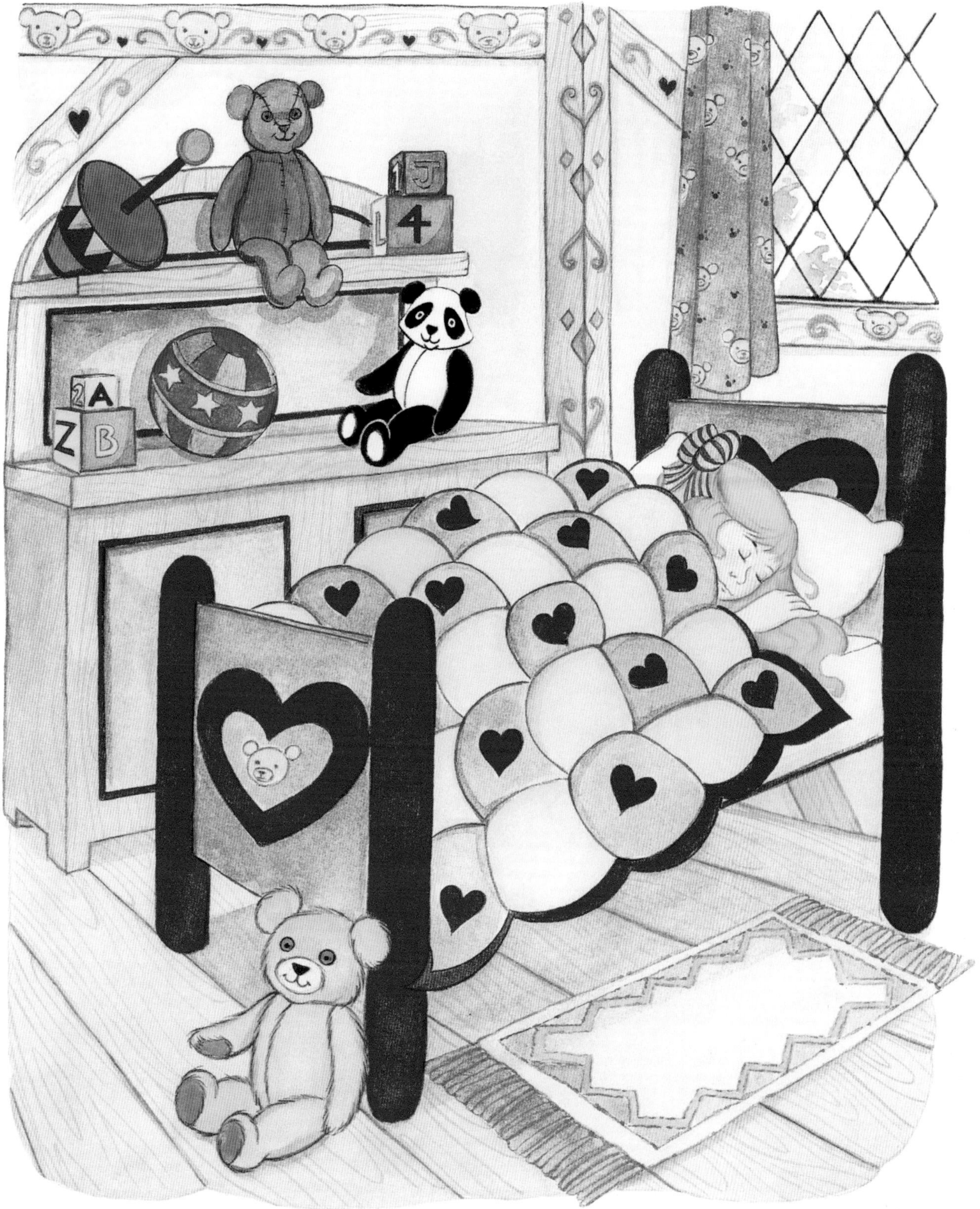

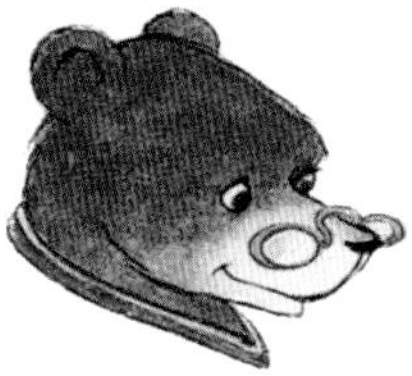 looked into his 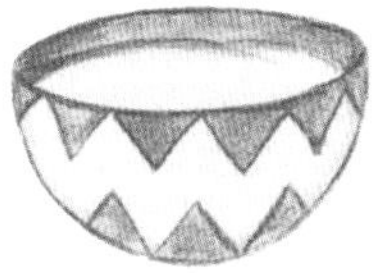.

"Somebody has been eating my porridge," he growled.

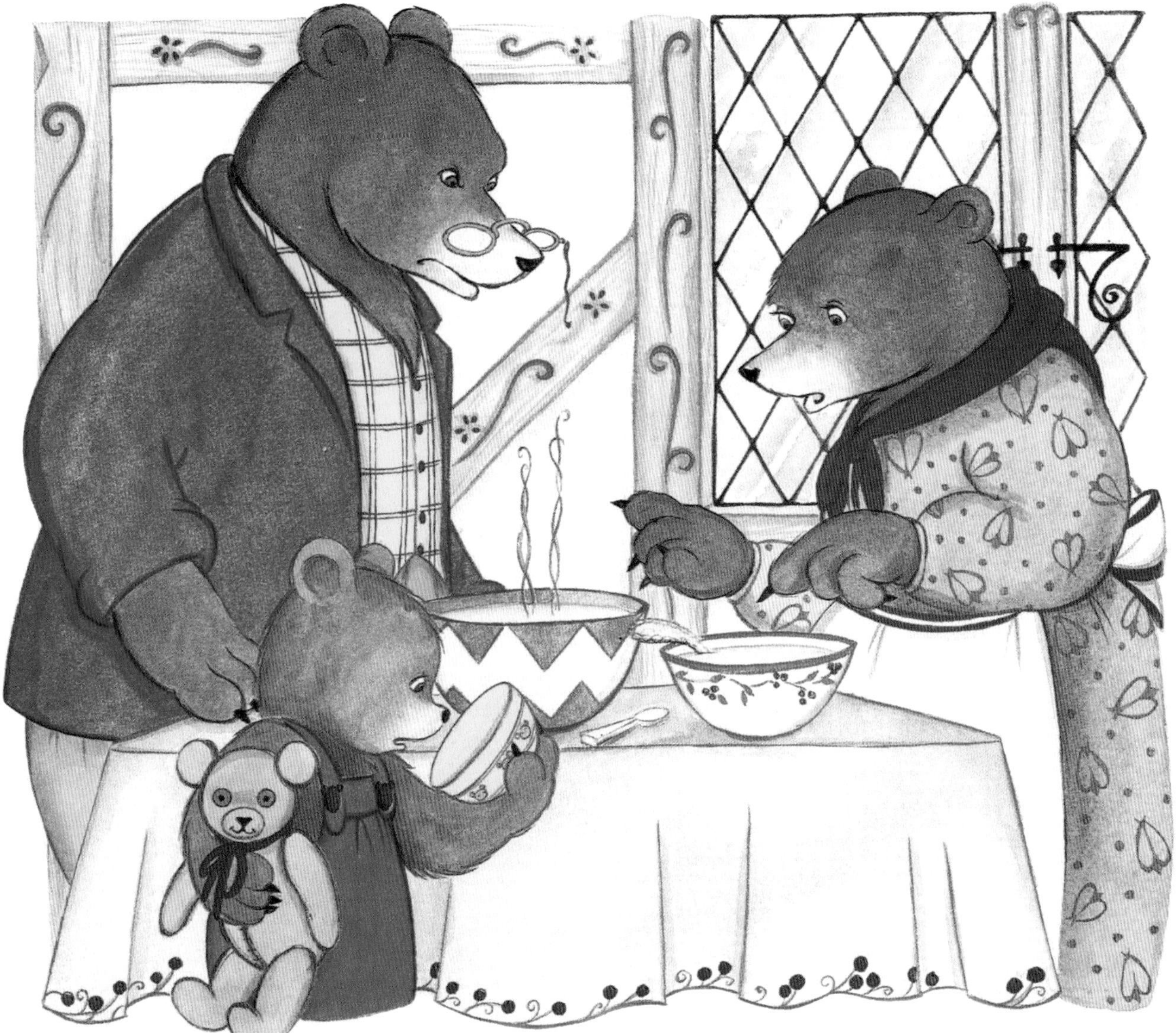

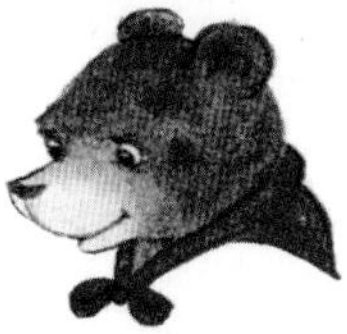 looked into her 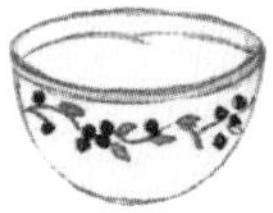,
with the 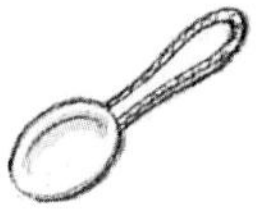 still resting in it.
"Somebody has been eating my porridge," she said in her middle-sized voice.

When poor 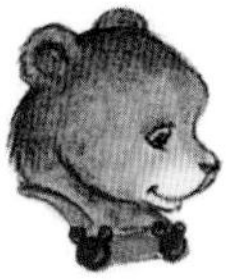 looked into his 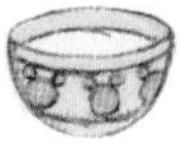 he found it was empty!

"Somebody has been eating my porridge," he cried in his squeaky little voice, "and it has all gone!"

 went to his 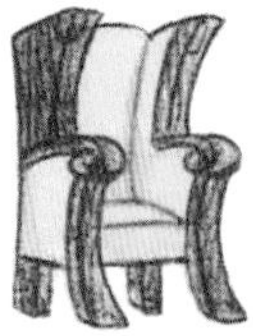 .

"Somebody has been sitting in my 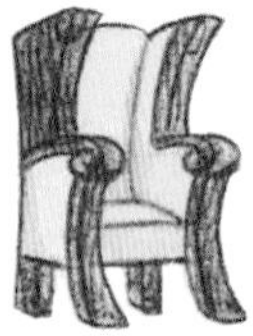 ," he growled in his big, deep voice.

"And somebody has been sitting in my  ," said   in her middle-sized voice. "The 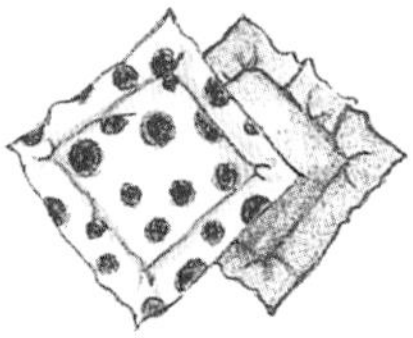 are all untidy."

When   looked for his  all he could see were  .

His little   filled with  .

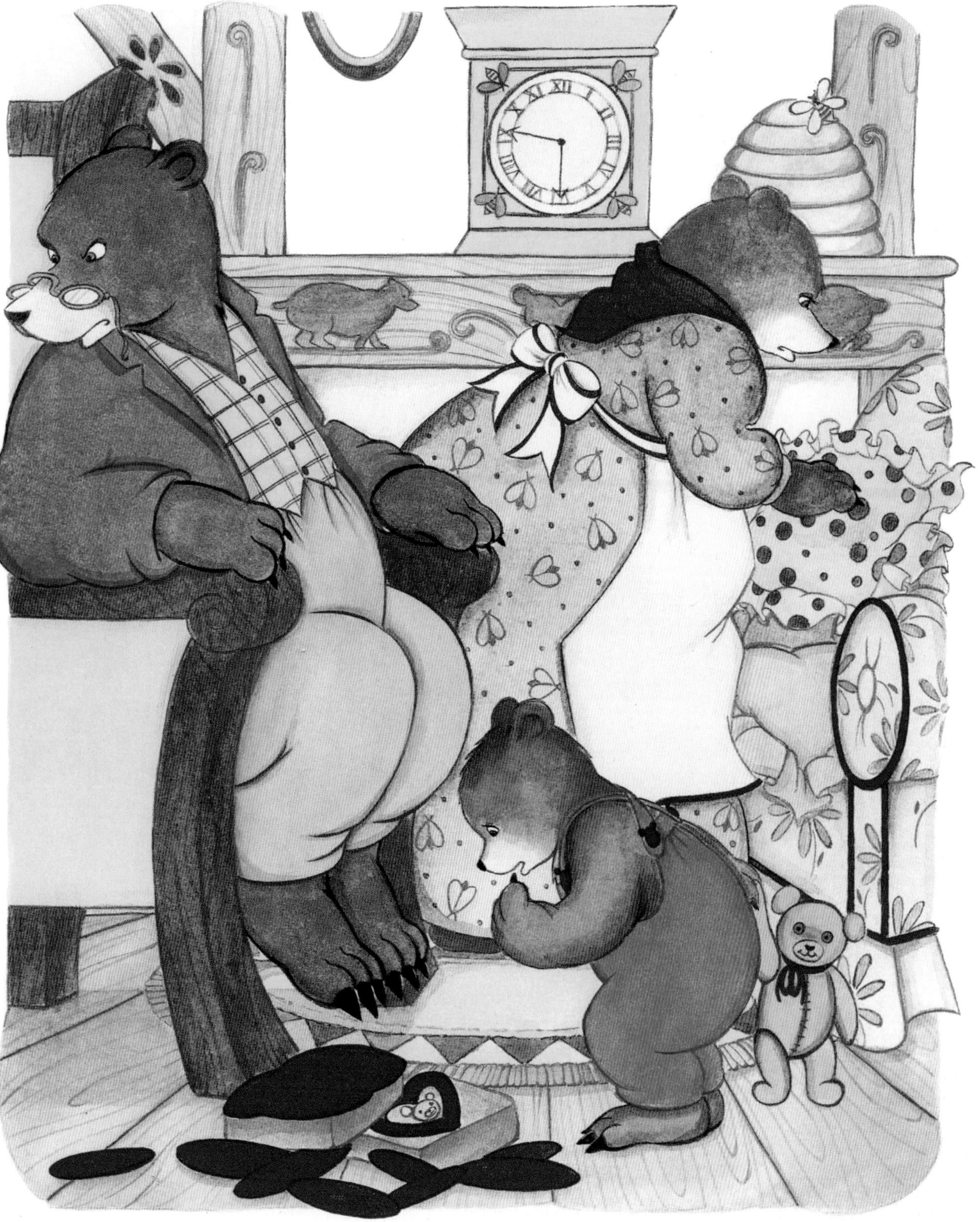

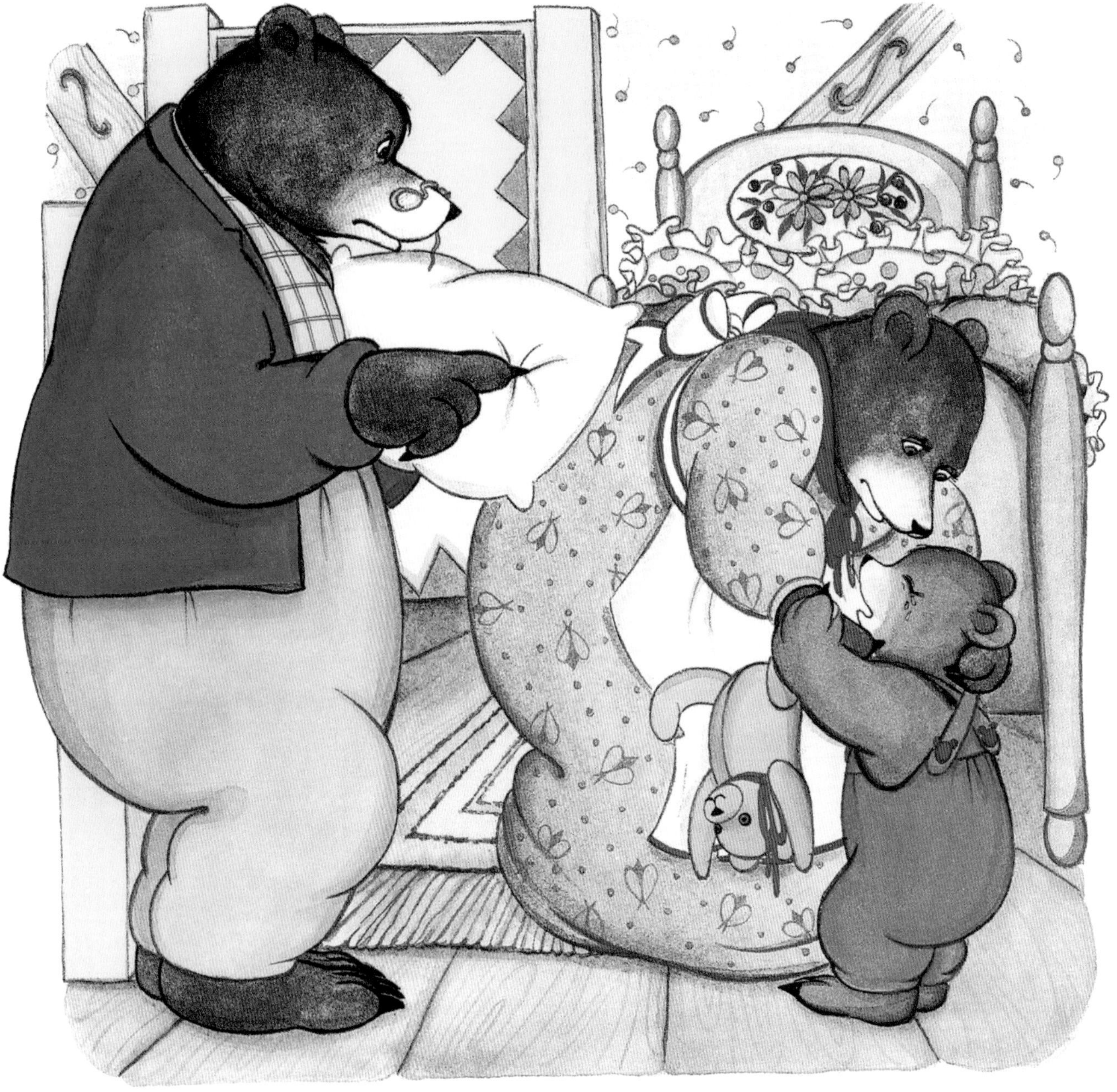

“Somebody has been sitting in

my 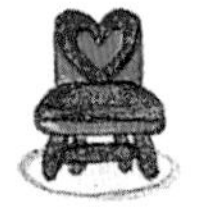 too,” he sobbed, “and it’s broken to 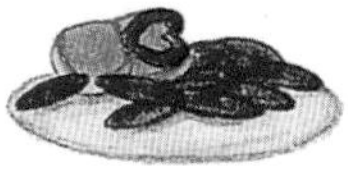 !"

The three 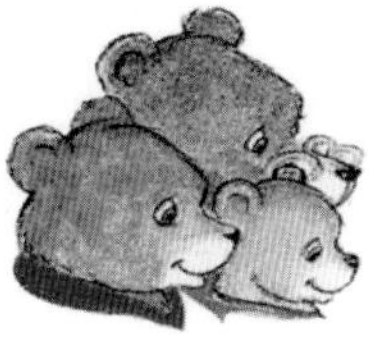 looked all over the room and under the 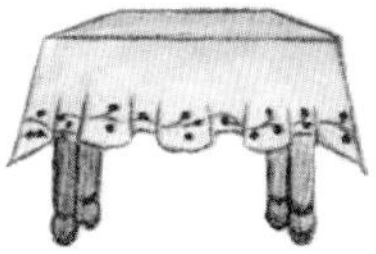 , but they could not find anyone.

Then they went up to look in the bedrooms.

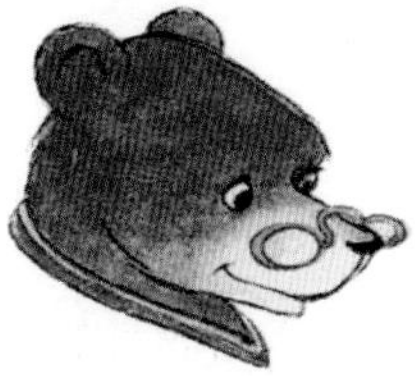 noticed that his 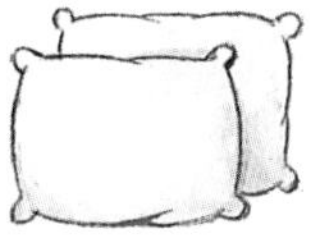 were all creased and untidy. "Somebody has been sleeping in my 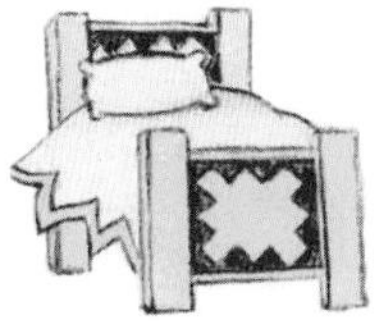 ," he called in his deep, gruff voice.

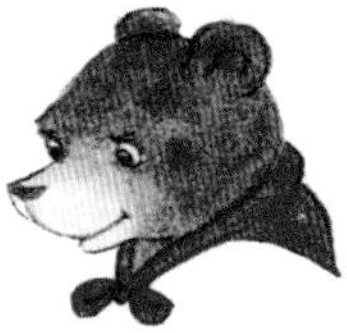 saw that her 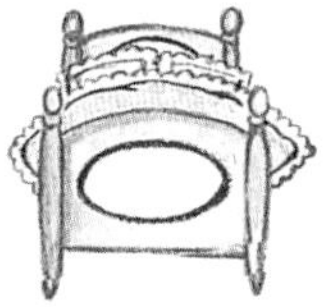 was rumpled. “Somebody has been sleeping in my 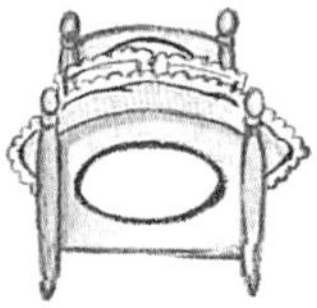,” she said in her middle-sized voice.

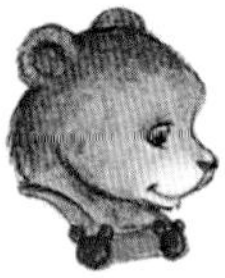 looked at his 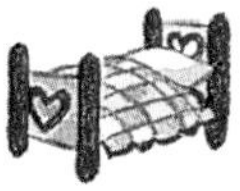. He could hardly believe his own 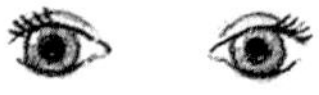. “There is somebody still sleeping in my bed!” he cried in his squeaky voice.

Just then, 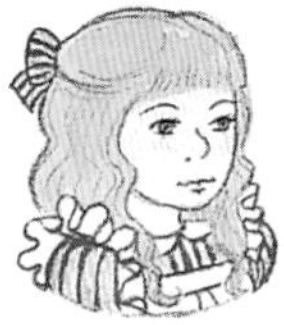 opened her 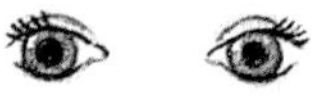 and saw the three 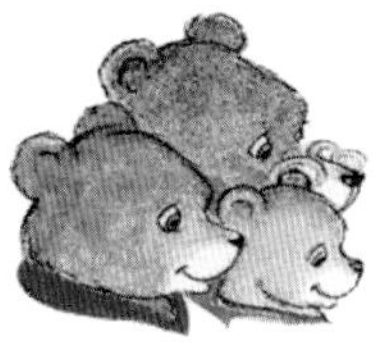.

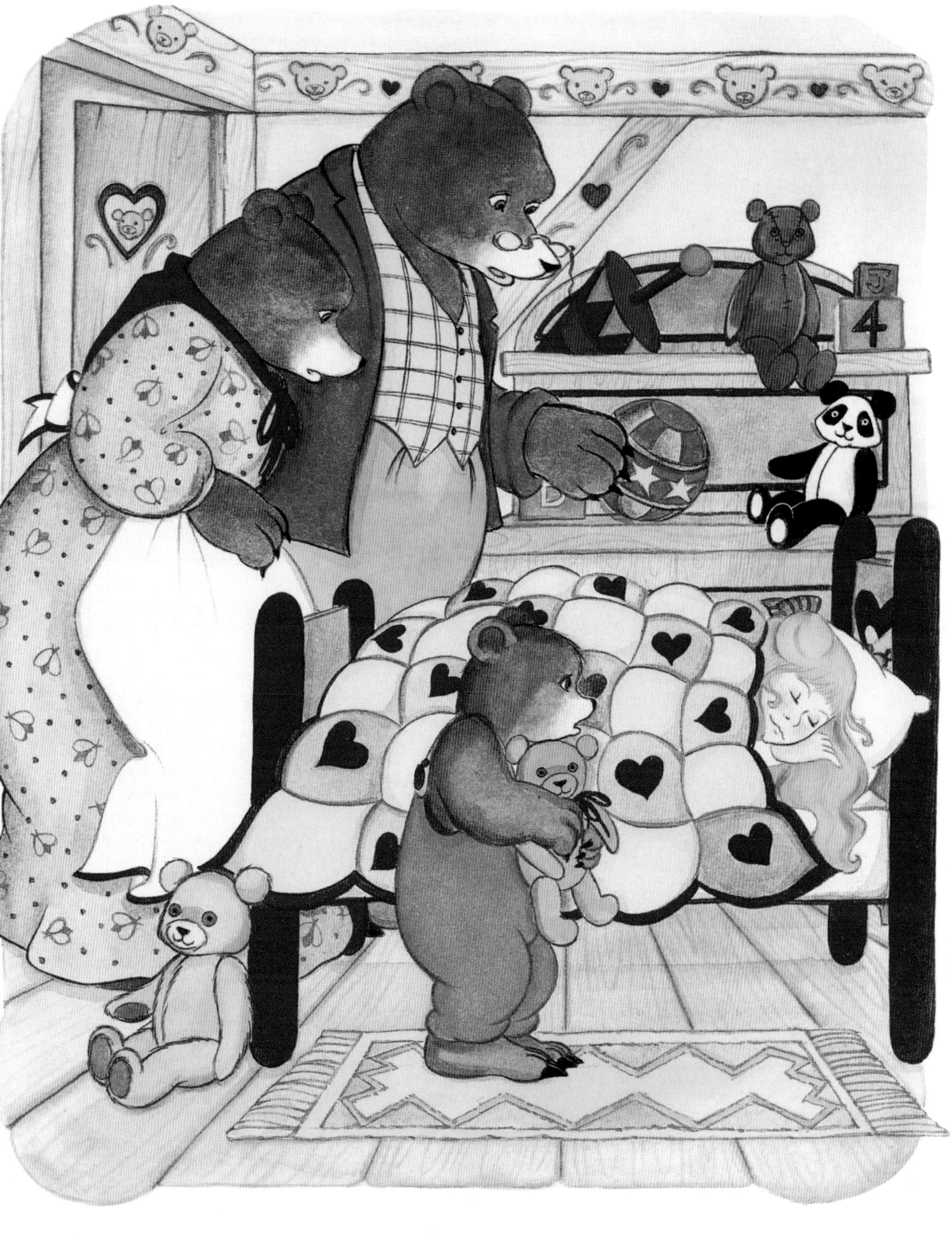
J
4

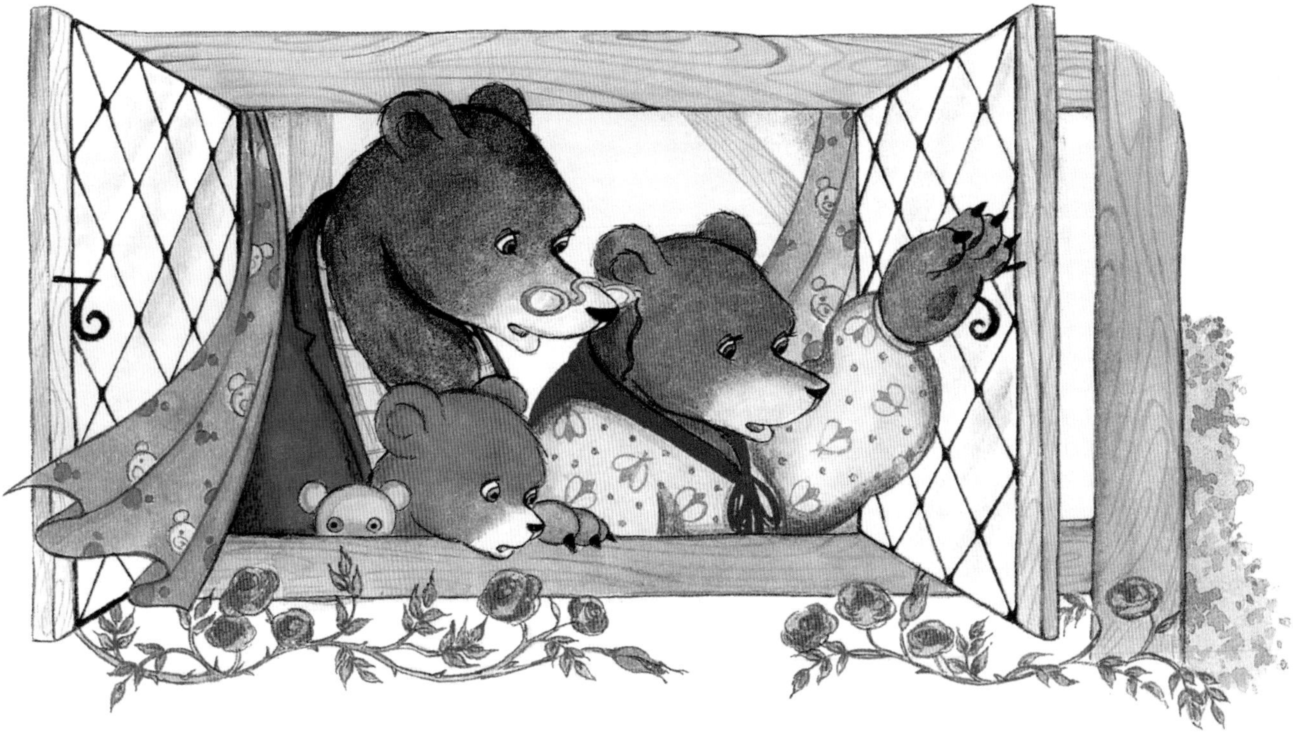

With a cry, 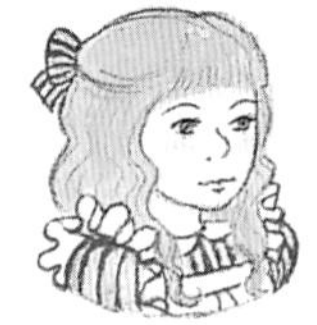 jumped out of the 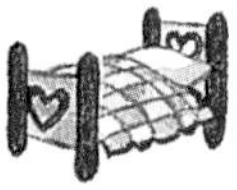. She ran down the 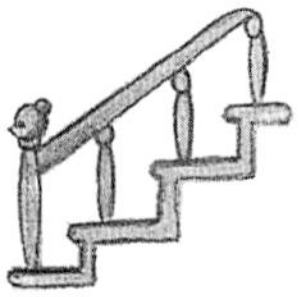, out of the 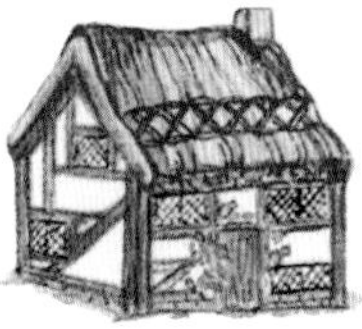 and into the 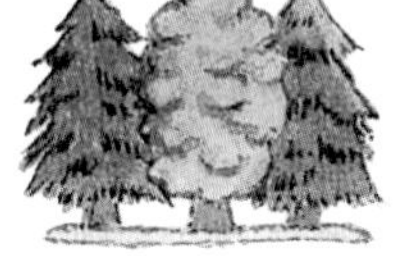.

"Please stop!" called the 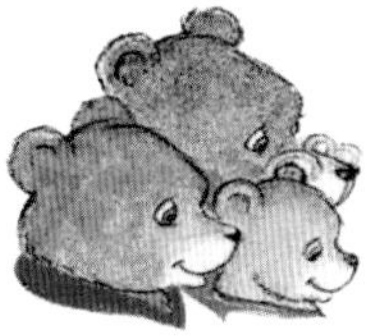. "We'll not harm you!"

But 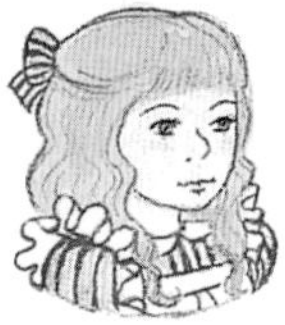 did not stop. She ran on through the 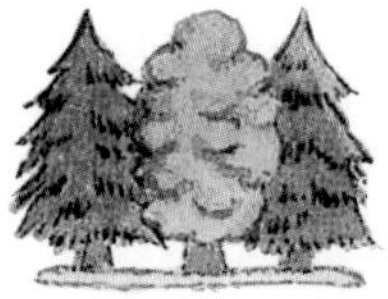 until she was safe in her own 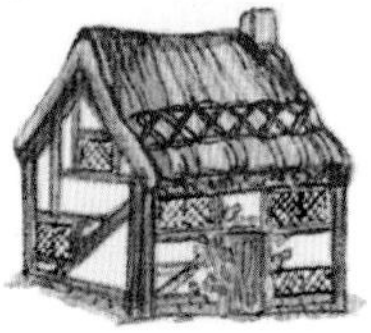 .

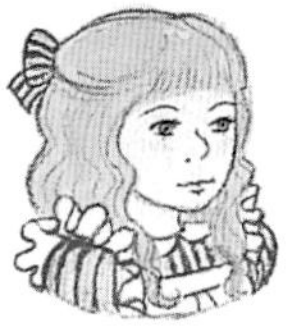 never went to visit the three 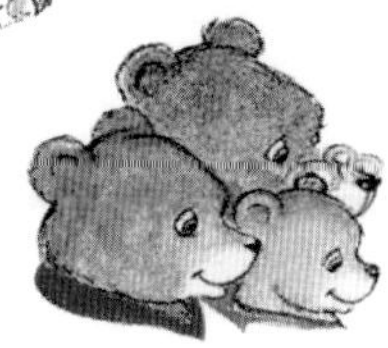 ever again.

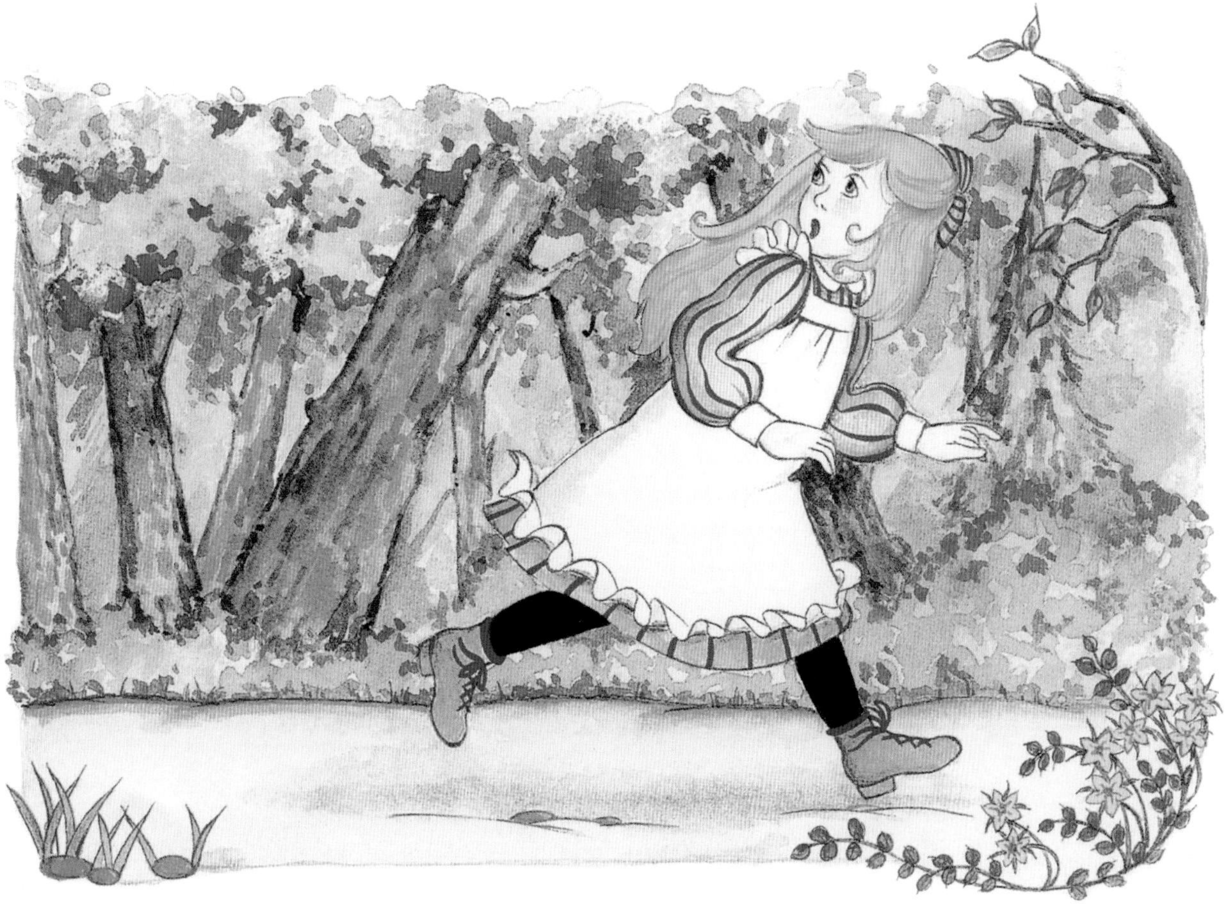

ISBN 978-1-78270-528-4 (paperback edition)
ISBN 978-1-78270-312-9 (book & CD edition)

Copyright © Award Publications Limited

Illustrated by Angela Hewitt

Book & CD edition
Audio recording ℗ 2008 Award Publications Limited
Story read by Sophie Aldred
Music composed by Tim King

Paperback edition first published 2022

Published by Award Publications Limited,
The Old Riding School, Welbeck,
Worksop, S80 3LR

 /awardpublications @award.books @award_books
www.awardpublications.co.uk

22-1032 1 (paperback edition)
22-1034 2 (book & CD edition)

Printed and made in China